Ready, Set, Oops!

by Fran Manushkin

illustrated by Diane Palmisciano

Kane Press, Inc.
New York

For Susan Green, and she knows why —F.M.

Acknowledgments: Our thanks to Rebecca Sawai, M.D., Oregon
Health & Science University, for helping to make this book as
accurate as possible.

Library of Congress Cataloging-in-Publication Data

Manushkin, Fran.
  Ready, Set, Oops! / by Fran Manushkin ; illustrated by Diane Palmisciano.
    p. cm. — (Science solves it!)
  "Life science/skin-Grades: K/2 ."
  "With fun activities!"
  Summary: Accident-prone Joey cannot think of an idea for Science Day until he becomes
inspired by all his scrapes and scabs.
  ISBN: 978-1-57565-246-7 (alk. paper)
  [1. Wounds and injuries—Fiction. 2. Science projects—Fiction. 3. Skin—Fiction.]
I. Palmisciano, Diane, ill. II. Title.
  PZ7.M3195Re2007
  [E]—dc22
                          2006102072

10 9 8 7 6 5 4 3 2

First published in the United States of America in 2007 by Kane Press, Inc.
Printed in U.S.A.

Book Design: Edward Miller

www.kanepress.com

"Mom, I need a Band-Aid!" I yell.

"Again? What happened this time, Joey?"

"I was jumping over a fire hydrant, and I tripped. No big deal."

Mom laughs. "You could break the world record for most Band-Aids in a day."

She's right. I bet I could!

"It wasn't my fault—this time," I say. "I was running to the library, and that hydrant just popped up out of nowhere!"

"Why were you running?" asks Mom.

"Because I need an idea for Science Day," I tell her. "And I need it *now.*"

"Get going, then. And take an extra Band-Aid."

"Won't need it, Mom." I grab a cookie instead.

I take off down the street and spot my friend Isabel on her porch. She's cooking eggs in a pizza box. How weird is that?

"Hey, Isabel," I ask, "is something the matter with your stove?"

"Nope," she says. "This is my Science Day project—the Sunny Sizzler 1000! It's a solar oven."

"You can cook eggs with the sun?" I ask.

"Piece of cake," Isabel says. "And today's perfect for it. The sun is really strong."

"No kidding." I wipe my face. "I'm so hot I could fry those eggs on my head!"

Isabel gives me a glob of sunscreen, and I scoot off down the street.

The sun can "cook" your skin. That's how you get a sunburn. Bad sunburns can even make people sick. Sunscreen keeps your skin from burning. It's very important! Use it every day.

Isabel's project is terrific. Everyone loves food! Food reminds me of my cookie, so I dig it out of my pocket. It's gooey, but good. I wish I had some nice cold lemonade to wash it down.

"Joey!" my friend Emmy calls. "Come check out my science project."

I put on the brakes.

"What's all this?" I ask Emmy.

"It's an experiment," she says, "to see if ice melts faster in salty water."

"That ice must be super cold," I tell her. "It's boiling out here, and you've got goosebumps!"

Your skin is working for you 24/7! If you're chilly, tiny muscles in your skin tighten up to keep the cold out. That's how you get goosebumps!

Emmy giggles. "And look—my fingers are all wrinkly, too." She hands me a few ice cubes, and I chew on them as I hurry away.

Your fingers can get wrinkly when they're in the water for a while. But don't worry—it just means your outer layer of skin is a little waterlogged. It'll snap back into shape soon after you dry off.

The ice cools me off, but a Double
Razzberry ice pop would cool me off even
more. I sure wish—

"Watch out!" yells my friend Steve.

CRASH! I run right into him and fall down.
Steve drops the box he was holding and balls
go flying all over the place. Steve, his sisters,
and their new puppy chase after them.

"What are you doing with all these basketballs?" I ask Steve.

"They're for my science project," he says. "I'm pumping them up with different amounts of air. I want to see how high each one will bounce!"

"Cool!" I tell him. "You'll be playing ball on Science Day. Why didn't I think of that?"

Steve's puppy starts sniffing my knee. His nose tickles and I laugh. "Hey, Rex—no scab sniffing!"

I glance at my watch. *"Yikes!* The library closes in an hour, and I still don't have a project idea. See you guys later!"

A scab is like a bandage your skin makes for you. It helps keep out germs and dirt while your body makes brand-new skin!

I hurry past my grandma's house and wave.
"Hi, Grandma!"

Whoosh! A gust of wind blows off her big
straw hat.

I jump as high as I can—and grab it!

"Good catch, Joey!" She gives me a thumbs up.

"And I didn't trip!" I say proudly.

Grandma puts her hat back on. "I'm keeping the sun off my face," she tells me. "I have too many freckles already."

"Your freckles are great," I say. "You wouldn't be Grandma without them."

> Everybody has something in their skin called **melanin**. The more you have, the darker your skin is. Sometimes melanin comes together in little spots, or freckles.

"Really?" Grandma is so pleased, she blushes.
"I like your blushes, too," I call as I dash off.

When blood rushes to the skin on
your face, it's called blushing. This
usually happens when someone is
embarrassed. Some people blush
more easily than others.

I pick up the pace. All this running is making me even hotter. Now I could use a Double Razzberry ice pop, a super-cold lemonade, and a mop to wipe up all this sweat!

Sweat is mostly water. It comes out of your body through tiny holes in your skin called **pores**. Sweat helps cool you off!

I see my friend Brooke carrying a bunch of petunia plants. I skid to a stop.

"What are you doing with those?" I ask.

"They're my Science Day project," Brooke explains. "I'm trying to find out if music makes plants grow faster."

"That's a great idea!" I tell Brooke. "Everyone likes music and flowers."

Brooke nods. "Bugs like my flowers, too. I think one just bit me."

"Mosquitoes *love* me," I say. "I get the biggest bites you ever saw."

I scratch one and rush off again.

A mosquito doesn't just "bite"—it injects spit into you! The spit makes it easier for the mosquito to suck your blood. Did you know that it's actually the spit that makes your skin red and itchy?

My friends have such cool projects. I've just
got to think of a—

Woo-hoo! I hear the jingle of the Mr. Freezie
truck. I'll bet I could think better if I had an
ice pop!

Everyone else wants ice cream, too. Isabel, Emmy, Brooke, my grandma, and Steve and his three sisters and Rex are all running toward the truck.

Steve buys four ice cream cones. He's so busy handing them to his sisters that he drops Rex's leash.

Just then a car zooms by. A big white poodle
is hanging out the window and barking.
Rex barks back and bolts toward the street.
"Stop, Rex!" Steve yells. "Come back!"
But Rex keeps going.

I dash to the curb and grab Rex just as he reaches the street. "Got you!" I shout.

Oops! I trip over his leash, and—SPLAT! I'm on the ground.

But I don't let go of Rex.

Everyone comes running.

"You saved Rex!" Steve says.

"Are you okay, Joey?" asks my grandma.

"Just a scraped knee," I tell her. "Do you have a Band-Aid?"

Grandma does, of course. "You're going to have another scab for your collection," she says.

Your skin and your brain make a great team! Whenever you touch something, a message is sent from your skin to your brain. Your brain tells you what you're feeling—whether it's a scraped knee or a puppy's wet nose.

Rex starts sniffing at my knees. "Cut it out, Rex. My scabs aren't that interesting—" I stop. "Wait! Maybe they are! I mean, why do we get scabs anyway?"

"And goosebumps," says Emmy.

"And bug bites," says Brooke.

"And freckles," adds my grandma.

I snap my fingers. "That's it!" I shout. "I've got my Science Day project!"

I head off to the library—right after I get my Double Razzberry ice pop.

I find out about sweating and freckles.
I write down some stuff about bug bites and goosebumps and how water makes skin wrinkly.

I read about scabs, too—even though I'm already an expert.

And I only get
two paper cuts.

My project is a big hit! Tons of people stop to look, and everyone is fascinated. Guess why? Everybody has skin!

Science Day

Music and Plants

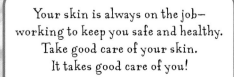

Your skin is always on the job—
working to keep you safe and healthy.
Take good care of your skin.
It takes good care of you!

THINK LIKE A SCIENTIST

I can observe and draw conclusions!

Joey thinks like a scientist—and so can you!

Scientists are like watchdogs—always on the lookout! They watch and listen to the world around them. Then they draw conclusions about the things they see and hear. For example, if you see a puppy pawing at a bag of dog food and howling, you might conclude that he wants his supper!

Look Back

- On page 8, what does Joey observe about Emmy?
- What does Joey observe about Rex on pages 12 and 26?
- On page 20, what does Joey observe his friends doing? What conclusion does he draw from what he sees?
- Look at page 30. What is Joey's project about? What does he observe on pages 26–27 that gives him this idea?

Try This!

Look at the pictures. What conclusions can you draw from observing Steve and Rex?

1. Why do you think Steve is inside?

2. What do you think he is going to do?

3. What do you think happened?